Puppy Love

Also by Anna Wilson

Pup Idol
Puppy Power
Kitten Kaboodle

Coming soon

Kitten Smitten

And chosen by Anna Wilson

Fairy Stories
Princess Stories

Anna Wilson

Puppy Love

Illustrated by MOIRA MUNRO

MACMILLAN CHILDREN'S BOOKS

First published 2008 by Macmillan Children's Books
a division of Macmillan Publishers Limited
20 New Wharf Road, London N1 9RR
Basingstoke and Oxford
Associated companies throughout the world
www.panmacmillan.com

ISBN 978-0-330-45289-2

7 9 8 6

A CIP catalogue record for this book is available from
the British Library.

Typeset by Nigel Hazle
Printed and bound in the UK by CPI Mackays, Chatham ME5 8TD

To Arvon, May 2007,
for inspiration and a lot o' larfs

Contents

1
How to Be Persistent

This is the story of how my wish came true. The wish that I, Summer Holly Love, have been holding close to my heart for all of my life – well, for as long as I can remember, anyway.

It's also the story of how my older sister, April Lydia Love, nearly wrecked my wish and (almost) made me wish I hadn't wished it, because of her totally weird and unforgivably embarrassing behaviour. More of that later.

Get on with the story!

It began when I started
YEARNING for my very
OWN pUppY to have
and to hold for ever
and ever, Amen.
And believe me,
I have prayed that a
million thousand times
to anyone who I
thought might be
listening. But for a long
time it didn't seem like
anyone was listening
AT ALL.

Like you're not listening to me now?

2

The funny thing about people not listening to you, I have found, is that they only don't listen when you're trying to tell them something important, like how much you are yearning for your very own pUppY! For example, when I used to ask Mum over and over again she never seemed to be listening at all, but always said, 'Hmm, maybe. Ask me again when I'm not driving around a roundabout/reversing into a blinking tight car-parking space.'

But then whenever I had to tell her things I'd rather not, like, 'I'm sorry I seem to have got extra homework again,' she was always on a totally different wavelength altogether and heard me vERY LoUD AND CLEAR INDEED.

Boy, are you long-winded

I have to say though, I am now living proof that it really pays off to be PERSISTENT, as Molly Cook, my best friend, would say. (Molly is great at using long words and then explaining them to you so that you can just NONCHALANTLY drop them into conversations to impress people when they are not expecting it.)

So, after being persistent about the puppy for the longest time ever, I got the

chance to be even more persistenter when a boy in my class called Frank

(who's OK most of the time as long as you don't sit next to him towards the end of the week because he only changes his

socks on a Monday, and, like, do they
start to honk by Wednesday afternoon)
said that his Labrador (who has the
unfortunate name of Meatball) had had
pUppIES!

At last! I thought you'd never
get there . . .

He brought in photos and everything.
And were those puppies CUTE or what?

Oh stop, this is getting
emBarrassing!

Mr Elgin even let Frank stand up in class
and tell us about the puppies being born,
and how he'd stayed up all night to
watch. And then Frank put on this kind
of serious voice you hear on the radio

5

when people are advertising things for sale and said:

Every puppy needs a good home, so if you are interested, please do not hesitate to contact me and arrange an appointment.

6

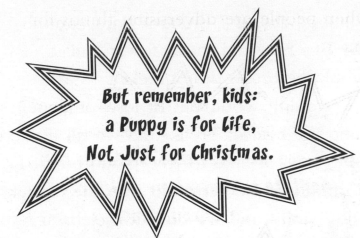

But remember, kids:
a Puppy is for Life,
Not Just for Christmas.

Which was a daft thing to say, as we'd only just had Easter. I even still had a stash of mini eggs left in my secret place under my bed behind my Celebrity Club folder, next to my torch.

At that point Mr Elgin said, 'Thank you, Frank, that will do. Go back to your place, please.' So Frank did.

After that I really couldn't concentrate on any lessons. I was just watching the clock on the wall, which definitely moves a lot slower than the one at home, and

7

thinking that if I thought hard enough
the hands would move faster and it
would be break time quicker.

It didn't work, but at last someone
rang the bell for break and we all made a
beeline for the playground. I
normally just go straight into the corner
with Molly and we do our Celebrity
Club, but today I had to have a Very
Important Appointment with Frank to
discuss the Puppy Situation. So that's why
I made the beeline.

Frank was kicking a ball around
as usual, so when I said, 'Frank, about
those puppies,' he didn't hear me.
Honestly, sometimes I just think I'm
INVISIBLE. So I made my beeline
right in front of him and
did a bit of nifty footwork
and got the ball off him

and passed it skilfully to one of his smelly
mates.

'Oi!' said Frank.

'Summer, actually,' I said, and I
folded my arms like Mum does when you
know she means business.

'What?' said Frank. Boys really are
the thickest sandwich in the picnic basket
sometimes. I tried again.

'I said, "About those puppies."'

'No, you didn't,' said Frank. 'You
said, "Summer actually."'

He's right, you did.

I raised my eyebrows and sighed in a
particularly dramatical manner and said,
'That's my name.'

'What are you on about?' said Frank.
It was then that I knew I had to

9

use my most Mum-like tone to get his attention. 'I want to talk to you about your puppies, Frank Gritter.'

'You'll have to make an appointment,' he said importantly and tried to get past me, back to his football-playing mates.

'I am making an appointment right now,' I said. This is how to be truly persistent, I thought.

Frank sighed and said, 'Come round after tea – but my mum says anyone interested has to have Parental Consent.'

I wasn't sure what Parental Consent was, but I thought that it must be something to do with parents, and that I could probably get anything I wanted now that I was in such a persistent frame of mood.

'OK,' I said, and stepped to one side

10

so that Frank could kick a ball around again and make his socks even more sweatier. I made a mental reminder not to stand too close to him at his house that night.

Did someone mention socky-whiff?
Mmmm, my favourite!

2
How to Get Parental Consent

I stared at those clock hands for the rest of the day, which meant I didn't get much out of the history lesson about the Victorians that we had in the afternoon, but to be totally honest I don't ever get much out of the history lessons we have about the Victorians. I know that the Victorians had a queen called Queen Victoria, which I always thought was quite clever of them, and I know that they invented penny-farthing bicycles, but frankly what use were they? I don't know anyone today who has even the slightest use for a penny-farthing bicycle. And even in the Victorian olden times only people with the most UNFEASIBLY long legs must have been able to ride them. So I don't get much out of the Victorians, personally. Especially when I'm thinking about how to get Parental Consent so that I can at last get my very own pUppY.

That's right – focus, kid, focus.

Someone in the school did finally decide to ring the bell for the end of the day (one day I will find out who this person is and

13

have a word with them to see if they can
ring it earlier, as all this waiting around for
the bell to ring is very tiring), so, without
waiting for Molly like I normally do, I
ran all the way home. And on the way
I started practising my very-well-planned
conversation that I'd made up in my head
during the history lesson. It went something
like this:

'Hello, Mum. That's a lovely dress
you're wearing. Oh, and your hair is
beautiful today. Did you
know that my friends
think you are the most
nicest-looking mum of
all the mums?'

At this point
Mum would
smile and
say, 'How lovely,

14

Summer. And may I say that you are looking most gorgeous today yourself?'

Then I would say, 'Mum, can I get you anything? Let me make you a cup of tea. You must have had a hard day.'

And I would lead her to a chair and sit her down and fetch some of those lemony biscuits which she loves but which she is always trying not to eat as they are 'so bad for the figure'. And then I'd make her a cup of tea while chatting in a friendly way about my day at school, which she always wants me to do, but which I never do because I'm always in a hurry to watch *Seeing Stars* on telly.

I have to say a bit about this show, because it is truly the most inspirationalist of shows I have ever seen on The Box (as Mum likes to call the telly, in that old-fashioned way of hers). It is a show which is a contest for people to become Celebrities, which is of course what my biggest AMBITION is. And because Molly is my best friend, it is her ambition too.

To enter this show it doesn't even matter what your talent is, you just have to have one. So you could be a brilliant singer, or a top dancer or a mega-magician or even just be really good at telling jokes. Then you get up on stage in front of what is called a Panel of Judges (although why it is called this I have no idea, as they are just people sitting behind a desk, and there is no panelling in sight at all) and you PERFORM.

If the person is very good, the judges are kind and lovely and say wonderful things about how great the performance is. If the person is bad, they say horrible things that I wouldn't even say to someone like Frank Gritter. They say, 'That was truly the worst dance I have ever had to sit through. You looked like a sack of potatoes on the back of a lorry driving down a bumpy road, and your dress looks like it's covered in cat sick,' or something like that. The person then has to try very hard not to cry because it is embarrassing on telly if you cry. (Unless you are supposed to because you are acting in a dramatical drama of some kind.)

Anyway, once the judges have said who
they like best, which is the bit which Molly
says is called 'Delivering the VERDICT',
we, the audience at home, get to vote BY
pHONING тHE ACτUAℓ SτUDιo!
Except I never can as Mum says the phone
bill would go through the roof if I did. (And
how on earth a phone bill is able to rocket
through bricks and tiles etc., I do not know.
Mum does say weird things.)

Anyway, because I cannot vote, Molly
and I decided to set up our own Celebrity
Club instead. And we do it after school
whenever we can, usually underneath
my bed which is one of those ones on a
platform where you have a desk under it.
Molly and I are going to be famous with
our Celebrity Club and we'll be on telly
with our own show just like the people on
Seeing Stars. One day.

But unfortunately for me, I was not a famous celebrity on the day in question, which was the day I was trying to get Mum to let me have a puppy. So instead of using my powers of celebrity, I had to use my powers of persuasion to get Mum to listen to me.

To go back to my very-well-planned conversation in my head, after telling Mum what a YUMMY MUMMY she was, the next thing I thought I would say in my friendly chatty manner was:

'A very interesting thing happened this morning at school, actually, because my charming friend, Frank Gritter, told us that his Labrador has had pUppIES and that we are all most welcome to come and see them after tea at his house. As long as we have Parental Consent.'

And then Mum would answer . . .

★

19

'Summer! What on earth have you got down your shirt?'

Mum had been spying on me running down the road and I had not noticed because my head was full of my very-well-planned conversational ideas. She had come out of the house and stopped me in mid-tracks. I screeched to a halt like people in cartoons do whenever they see a seriously bad Baddie and blurted out:

'Hello, Mum. That's a lovely skirt/dress/T-shirt you're wearing—' Whoops. Forgot to delete as applicable.

 Not your smartest move, I have to say . . .

'What?' She closed her eyes and shook her head. She always does this when I say something she considers to be silly. She

sighed, gave me a kiss, then turned to go
into the house and I followed her down
the hall.

I decided to try out my very-well-
planned conversation, so I went into the
kitchen and threw my bag and pakamac
down by the radiator, which is my usual
place for putting my things as I can always
find them then.

Mum sighed noisily and went to pick
up my bag but I put my hand on her arm
in a gentle and concerned fashion and said,
'Come and sit down
and I'll make you a
nice cup of tea. You
must have had a hard
day.'

Mum's eyes did
something very strange then.
They looked as if they were going

21

to pop out of her head, and I'm sure she actually stopped breathing. But she did go and sit down. Good thing really. If she had actually stopped breathing in true life she might have fainted, and I couldn't let that happen before I had asked her about the pUppIES.

Too right, sister!

I made a lovely cup of tea and got the lemony biscuits.

Mum narrowed her eyes at the biscuits. 'What are you up to, Summer?' she said in a suspicious manner. 'Oh, put those biscuits away – they are so bad for the figure.'

She ate three while I started to tell her in a pleasant and chatty way about my day and how Molly and I had played with Rosie Chubb in first break, but then

How to Get Parental Consent

Rosie Chubb had got in a mood with us because we wouldn't tell her about our club, so she poked a pencil in Molly's arm and Molly had to go to the Welfare Room to see whether or not we would have to call an ambulance. I had personally thought an ambulance would definitely be needed, as I had seen on telly that you could get lead poisoning if lead got in your skin or blood or something. Molly had said she was positive she would need a blood test to check her Heemi-Goblins Level. At least, I thought that's what she said, but she was doing that hiccuping crying she does when she's really panicky so I hadn't been able to hear very well what she was saying. (Actually, she can't have said that, as how can there be goblins in your blood?)

But the nurse said we were Making

a Fuss and that
pencils don't have
real lead in any
more. So at lunch
we decided to
break up with
Rosie Chubb
because she couldn't be our friend if she was
going to stick pencils in us that weren't even
real lead, and anyway by that time a more
interesting thing had happened which was,
'. . . my charming friend Frank telling us
about his dog's puppies—'

Mum choked a bit on the last crumbs of
her third lemony biscuit and said in a rather
strangled voice, 'Oh no!'

'Are you all right?' I asked in my
most anxious and worried tone. Maybe
the biscuits had started to upset her figure.
'Should I call a doctor?'

'NO!' Mum bellowed, coughing and spluttering. 'I should have known you were up to something.'

'Me?' I said, pointing at my chest and making my eyes do that wide innocent thing people do on telly when they can't believe someone is saying that they've done something they very much obviously have.

'Yes, YOU, young lady. You're trying yet again to get me to agree to having a dog. Well, I won't. Ever.'

Wow, she's one tough lady.

I felt a little tiny-weeny bit cross at this. That's the last time I make tea and get out the lemony biscuits and chat about my day, I thought. But then I remembered that I was supposed to be being persistent and getting Parental Consent, so instead of sulking and saying, 'It's not fair,' I said in my grown-up-discussion voice, 'I don't really understand why you are so unkeen on the idea.'

'Because it would end up being *my* dog,' she said.

I'm sure Mum and I speak a different language most of the time: I was asking for my very *own* puppy, so in what way would it end up being *Mum's* dog? So I asked her, 'Excuse me, Mum, but in what way would it end up being *your* dog?'

'In the way that *I* would be the one clearing up after its mess, *I* would be the one taking it for walks and *I* would be the one taking it to the vet,' Mum said in, I have to say, a quite unpleasant tone of talking.

'But you wouldn't!' I protested. 'I'm totally brilliant at going for walks and clearing up messes.'

26

'Huh!' Mum did a half-snort and a grunt. Not very attractive, in my opinion.

You should hear yourself sometimes, kiddo . . .

'Listen,' I said trying to sound soothing and sensible. 'I *promise* I would take it out for a walk every day before school. And I'd get one of those super-duper pooper-scooper things to clear up any mess it makes,' I said, smiling like an angel.

'Summer,' she said in her most DECISIVE and scariest way, 'I remember you saying similar things about the stick insects, before they mysteriously disappeared. In fact, whatever happened to them . . . ?'

Here we go yet again, I thought wearily. But I tried not to look wearily and kept the angelical smile on my face. It was beginning to feel a bit stiff. (By the way, I'm sure I never promised to take the stick insects for a walk every day.)

'And what about the cats?' she was still wittering on. 'Who feeds them every day and picks up all the dead mice and birds they bring in through the cat flap?'

'You do,' I admitted, smiling carefully, 'but I never wanted the cats anyway.'

I probably shouldn't have said that last bit, but it was totally true. *Mum* had always wanted cats. I think she thought that if she got

cats then I'd forget all about how much I
yearned for a $p\bigcup pp$Y. But the thing is,
Cheese and Toast're not that much fun now
they're not kittens. They just sleep all day
and go out all night. (Sometimes I actually
wish I was a cat. I would have a nice life,
and I certainly wouldn't have to learn my
seven times table.) Besides, they are not
very cuddly and the only lap they'll sit on is
Mum's.

 Yup. They're dull, dull dull.

'Oh, come on, Mum, pur-*leeese*!' I had given
up on the smile by now and was doing that
thing when you've got your hands between
your legs as if you desperately need to go to
the loo and my eyes were tight shut and I
was doing what I think is called a Grimace,
in other words my mouth was stretched in

29

an expression of complete AGONY and I was showing all my teeth. I was also whining. I think I looked like what Molly calls an Utter Nutter, I'm embarrassed to say. '*Please* give me Parental Consent and come with me to Frank's and have a look at them.'

'Oh, anything to stop you pulling those bizarre faces,' she said grudgingly. And I'm sure she almost smiled.

I could feel my eyes going shiny and I felt BUBBLY WITH EXCITEMENT. I jumped up to give her a hug and disastrously knocked her teacup flying. This was not a good move and totally definitely not part of my very-well-planned conversation.

How to Get Parental Consent

She threw a cloth at me and cried,
'Before we go anywhere, you'd better prove
how good you are at clearing up messes!'

The thing about mums is, they always get
the last word.

3
How to Be Persuasive

I chewed my nails all the way to Frank's. I had promised myself never to chew my nails again because I know it is not what celebrity people do, and Molly says that if we are going to Get Anywhere with our Celebrity Club, we must not bite our nails any more. So I had painted them with this shiny stuff which I thought looked Glam and Gorgeous like the real nail varnish my sister, April, wears but it actually tastes Grim with a capital G! There is one problem I have found though. If you are truly stressed and anxious about something,

you will always find a way to stop thinking
about the Grim taste and you will always bite
your nails anyway. So that's what I was
doing on the way to Frank's house.

I just kept thinking and turning it over
in my head: 'What if the whole class has
already been there and all the puppies have
gone? What if Frank laughs at me and says,
'Ha ha! You are too late, Summer Holly
Love!' and what if there's not much room
in the room and I have to stand too close
to him and try not to be sick because of
the smell of his socks? Because if I was sick
because of the smell of his socks, he might
be angry and not let me take one of the
puppies. And what if Mum just takes one
look at the puppies and says, 'NO WAY
HO-ZAY,' like they do in films and then
Frank laughs and says, 'I told you you
needed Parental Consent!'

33

'Does Frank's mother know we are coming to look at these puppies?' Mum asked, breaking her way into my most anxious thoughts.

Why do mums always worry about other mums knowing whether you are coming round or not? Molly's mum, Mrs Cook, is always happy to see me whenever I turn up and she says, 'It's nice to see you girls playing together,' and she always gives us flapjacks with apricots in, which she knows are my favourite.

I just shrugged and said, 'Frank said to come round.'

Mum sighed and muttered something about 'getting this over and done with'.

I rang the bell and we waited. I thought we might hear yapping or barking as Frank said there were eight puppies, but there was not a sound of a dog at all.

Frank opened the door and Mum took a
step back. The sock smell was particularly of
a whiffy nature.

Yum!

I held my breath and tried to speak quickly
so that I wouldn't have to breathe in the
honking smell.

'Hello, we are here because I have got
Parental Consent to have an appointment
with you about the puppies.'

Frank grinned and led us into his house.
His mum was in the kitchen. I was really
very surprised to see that she was quite
clean and normal-looking. She did not smell
of socks at all. The kitchen was even tidier
than our own, in actual fact.

Mum had got her 'Isn't this nice? I'm
ever so delighted to be here' smile on. The

mums started a chat about school and how lovely it was that they had children in Year Four now and what a difference it made.

I didn't know how much of a difference it could make to anyone what year we were in, but mums are always saying things like this. Molly says she thinks it's all a secret language that only mums understand. They say these things to each other that we think are dull and make no sense, but then they always seem to have picked up all kinds of information that we don't want them to have about our lives. And they always say they got it from someone else's mum. Maybe the government gives you a secret handbook when you become a mum that tells you the language so you can learn it in time for your children to start school. Governments do that kind of thing. I've seen it on telly.

Anyway, Frank did a circly thing with his eyes and beckoned to me to follow him. He obviously thought that mum-conversations are totally baffling and dull too. We went out of the kitchen into the room where the washing machine was. I hoped he wasn't going to ask me to wash his socks while I was there.

'Why are we in here?' I asked. 'I thought you were going to show me the puppies.'

'They're in here, stupid,' said Frank. He obviously does not know that to be a truly successful sales-person you have to be charming and polite. Not rude and smelly.

He pointed to a large box in the corner of the room. I heard a small snuffling noise and rushed over to have a look. I could *not* believe what my eyes were telling me. On the far side of the box, snuggled up

37

against Meatball, were the tiniest, cutest, squidgiest *p*U*pp*IES ever in the whole world!

We pups aim to please . . .

'Why have they all got their eyes closed?' I asked Frank, as I suddenly felt a little bit confused.

'Don't you even know *that*?' Frank asked in his huffy, girls-are-the-stupidest voice.

I felt my face going a bit red and hot which I don't like as it doesn't go extremely

well with the colour of my hair which is
what I like to call auburn, but my sister,
April, calls ginger.

'Well, they're very much obviously not
asleep, are they?' I said importantly. 'I can
see with my own eyes that they are moving
around – unless they are sleepwalking?'
I asked, feeling pleased with myself for
coming up with this brilliant explanation.

'Duh, stupid – they *can't* open their eyes,'
he said with what can only be described
as a very smug, know-it-all grin on his
unattractive features.

I put my hands on my hips to show
that I was not a girl to be messed with
or talked to in that manner. 'In that case,
Frank Gritter, you have broken the Sales
and Tradespersons Description Act,' I said
importantly. (Luckily I knew about this
because Molly told me that if you are

selling something you have to be truthful about all the details of what precisely you are getting, otherwise the government can put you in prison.) 'Who wants a puppy who can't open its eyes?'

'Oh, shut up,' said Frank. 'These little guys can't open their eyes because they are not even two weeks old. You would know this if you had been listening to what I said this morning. They are still being weaned. They should open their eyes any day now. That's why you can't take one home yet, even if you definitely want one and have definitely got Parental Consent. You can have one at seven or eight weeks. They'll be ready at half-term actually.'

I made a mental reminder to go and look up what 'weaned' meant. And also to check in a book whether or not Frank was telling the truth about the puppies not being

able to open their eyes yet. I did not want
to be sold a dog who could not fetch a stick
or a ball. How would I teach it tricks if it
could not see? I could not be a Responsible
Dog-Owner-Type person if I could not
train my dog. Anyway, I certainly was not
going to ask Frank about my Concerns, as
it would show that I was a tiny bit ignorant
of dog-type Issues, and then he might not
think I would be a suitable owner of a
pUppY.

Well, the thought did cross
my mind . . .

'Can I hold one?' I asked.

He reached into the box and picked up
one of the puppies. 'It's a girl,' he said.
A golden girl.

Frank put her into my arms. I could

almost have held her in one hand only.
And I nearly squealed when I touched her.
She was the MOST ABSOLUTELY
SOFTEST and VELVETEST thing you
have ever imagined. And she made small
grunty piggy noises that made me want

to squeal even more. But I didn't want to frighten her, so I just kept the squeals inside and gently stroked her.

That was when Mum and Mrs Gritter came in.

'So here's the whelping box,' said Mrs Gritter.

'Whelping': another word I absolutely had to remember to look up later.

'As I said, the puppies can't leave their mother yet, but if you want to put your name down for one, we can arrange for you to come back in a few weeks.'

I looked up at Mum, all ready to be most pERSUASIvE AND pERSISTENT. I had decided I wanted the puppy I was holding more than even I wanted to be the winner on *Seeing Stars*, and I was most determined to let Mum know this. But I didn't have to.

Mum looked at me holding Honey (that's what I knew I had to call her) and opened her mouth to say something like, 'We'll let you know,' which is her usual way of telling people that she's not interested. Then Honey stretched in my arms and sort of yawned in a very definitely cute kind of way.

Thanks, I thought so too!

Then Mum's face went a funny blotchy red.

She closed her mouth.

Then she opened it again.

Then she raised her eyebrows, sighed loudly and finally said:

'Isn't she gorgeous?'

I think in the end Honey was more persuasive herself than I could ever have possibly been on my own.

You said it, girl!

4
How to Be Prepared

So that was it – Mum couldn't go back on her word now. I was SO OVER THE MOON WITH GLEE AND HAPPINESS that I called Molly and told her about it straight away. She was OVER THE MOON too and said Honey could be an Honourable Member of our Celebrity Club, because lots of famous people have famous pets. Especially dogs, which they carry under their arm when they go shopping. (Although that would be a difficult thing to do with a fully grown-up Labrador.)

Then, because I was still
hyper-excitable, as soon as my
sister April came home I very
speedily filled her in on all the
details too. April is older than
me – twenty-two or some other
ancient age – and works in
town for an office of people who
are lawyers and they are called
Stingy and Gross. Apparently
lawyers are always called
something like Stingy and
Gross. Never Mr Stingy
and Ms Gross, just Stingy
and Gross. Molly says it's so you know they
are lawyers and not normal human beings.

(Molly and I don't want to work in
town when we are older, because when
we're older we're going to be famous, of
course, and go on telly about our Celebrity

Club and tell everyone how we shot to fame
in an important and glamorous manner
by winning all the votes in *Seeing Stars*. So
probably then we'll be so famous we won't
have to live at home with our mums any
more like my sister April does; we'll live in a
pent-flat suite, I expect.)

'April, we're getting a *pUppY*!' I
screamed. This was how I very speedily
filled her in on all the details.

'Typical,' she said, with an older-sister
SOPHISTICATED sigh. 'I start life in the
working world, and *you* get a puppy.'

She says that about everything. When
we got the new big flat telly with all the
different channels she said, 'Typical. I start
life in the working world and *you* get a
digital plasma telly,' and when we went to
Spain for a holiday last year without her
because she said she wouldn't be seen dead

on holiday with her 'baby sister', she said,
'Typical. I start life in the working world
and *you* go to Spain.' What does she expect?
Life doesn't stop because April Love's Started
Life in the Working World. That's what
Mum says, and I agree.

The thing is, it probably is a bit unfair,
because I know that April wanted a puppy
when she was still at school, but Mum
always put her foot down about it. But then
April probably didn't ever have a friend at
school whose dog had just had puppies so
that she could take Mum to see them. In
fact, I don't know if April had any friends
at all at school anyway.

Ouch! You're Bad!

When April had stopped doing her
sophisticated sighing she said she would like

to take me shopping at the weekend to get some stuff for Honey. I was actually quite shocked by how really kind and helpful this was, as April is not usually that interested in doing things with me.

But when I told Mum she laughed and said, 'April's such a shopaholic she'd go shopping for bags of mud if that was all there was left on the planet.'

As I have already explained, Mum is well known for saying the weirdest things.

Bags of mud sound good to me!

On the way back from Frank's house the night before, I had kept on thanking Mum over and over again for saying yes to having Honey. She had

smiled, but I could tell she was wondering
why on earth she *had* said yes, because
she put on a sort of stern face and said, 'I
haven't forgotten your part of the bargain,
Summer. You are going to help out with
this animal. I don't want to end up doing
all the work, even if I do think Honey's
sweet.'

Mrs Cook once told me that when there
is Tension in the Air, people often DE-FUSE
THE TENSION by telling a joke. I thought
it would be a good idea to have a go at
doing this myself.

'You are so funny, Mum!' I said.

'Eh?' said Mum.

'"Honey's sweet!" Haha!
Geddit?'

Mum groaned. But I think
at least the Tension was now De-Fused,
as she didn't say any more about how

51

much hard work it would be to have
Honey.

Hard Work? Me?

Anyway, she was right, I had
promised to help. So before the weekend
I thought I'd better Be Prepared for the
shopping trip and find out about exactly
all the special equipment a new puppy
needs.

I asked Molly the next day at school. I
didn't want to ask Frank as it was becoming
clear he was such an annoyingly know-it-
all dog-owner type, and anyway, I wanted
to steer clear, as it was Friday so the sock
aroma would be at its peak.

Molly and I were both already big fans
of the telly programme about training your
dog called *Love Me, Love My Dog*, which is

presented by a very scary-looking woman
who dresses from her top to her toes in
black shiny leather. Her name is Monica
Sitstill. She speaks in a teachery voice and
is always telling off bad owners for not
training their dogs properly. It is a funny
programme to watch, until you start to
think that you could end up being one of
those bad owners who can't train their dogs,
and then it doesn't seem quite so Amusing.
I would not like Monica Sitstill to come to
my house and talk in that teachery way to
me.

You and me Both . . .

'Monica Sitstill has written a book which
is all based on her programme, you know,'
said Molly. Molly knows everything about
everyone who's famous. That's why she

started the Celebrity
Club in the very first
place.

Celebrity Club

I gasped. '*Has* she?
Then I must get it. It
will tell me how to Be Prepared for my new
vERY oWN pUppY and how to train
her.'

'Indeed,' agreed Molly. 'Let's go to the
library at lunchtime and get a copy, then
we can start Making A List.'

Molly loves making lists. She says that
it is the only way in life that a girl can
be EFFORTLESSLY EFFICIENT. And it's
what famous people do. That's why they
never miss a party and always remember
never to wear the same dress more than
once at any one Celebrity Event.

So we went to the library and got a
copy of the book, which was also called

Love Me, Love My Dog. It had a picture on the front of Monica Sitstill in a black leather outfit as usual and she was pointing out of the cover as if she was pointing at me, which I did find rather scary, and there was a huge dog sitting at her feet and gazing up at her in an adoring manner. The photo proved that she is obviously a very good trainer of dogs indeed if she can train a dog that big.

This was the list we made:

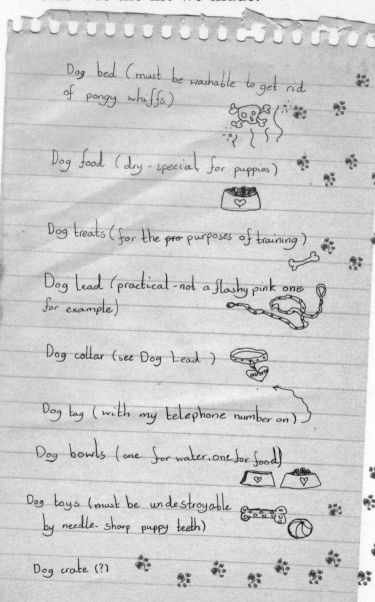

Dog bed (must be washable to get rid of pongy whiffs)

Dog food (dry - special for puppies)

Dog treats (for the ~~pro~~ purposes of training)

Dog lead (practical - not a flashy pink one for example)

Dog collar (see Dog Lead)

Dog tag (with my telephone number on)

Dog bowls (one for water, one for food)

Dog toys (must be undestroyable by needle-sharp puppy teeth)

Dog crate (?)

Pongy whiffs — YUM!

Sounds . . . er . . . mouthwatering
(NOT!) . . .

Now we're talking! (But what
is this 'training'?)

TOYS! TOYS! TOYS!

??? ! ! !

A dog crate was a very expensive thing, and I didn't know what Mum would think about this, so I made a mental reminder to ask her before I gave April the list on Saturday and let her Run Riot with Mum's credit card. Apparently April is always Running Riot with Mum's credit card, given half the chance.

When Mum says this I always get a very strange and funny picture in my head of April snatching Mum's card and sprinting off down the street like an Olympic-style athlete, shouting loudly at the top of her head and throwing bottles and things at police officers. I'm sure that's what a riot is, because it's what you see on the news sometimes, but I don't think April would really Run Riot like this as it would mess up her long blonde straight hair.

When we had finished the list I asked Molly if she would like to come shopping with me and April, and she said, 'Do the stars shine at night?'

Which is Molly's way of saying, 'You betcha.'

In other words – yes.

5
How to Use Your Initiative

The weeks between seeing
Honey for the first time and
finally bringing her home to live
with me for ever and ever
were the longest weeks I
have had to live through
in my whole long life. I truly
honestly do not know how I survived.
But Molly helped me through it
by phoning and coming
round lots

and lots to talk about Honey and
sort out the things we had
bought for her and get the
house ready.

Molly and I read the *Love Me, Love
My Dog* book about a million thousand
times until I could actually quote chunks
of it off by heart. I learned that 'weaning'
is when the puppy starts to eat proper
puppy food and stops having so much of its
mother's own milk, and that a 'whelping
box' is where the puppies are born and
stay until their eyes have opened and they
can walk. Mum started off being ever so
impressed by my instant recall of all dog-
related facts and figures, but I think in
the end I might have annoyed her ever so
slightly.

You don't say . . .

'Summer – that's enough! I know
you have to de-worm a puppy
dog every four weeks, I know
they can't be left on their own for
more than an hour to start with,
and I know that I'm beginning to seriously
blinking regret saying you could blinking
have the blinking animal in the first blinking
place!'

Hmm. Mum was getting a bit stressed
and anxious about what Life With Honey
was going to be like, so I did my best to
calm her and reassure her that I knew what
I was doing and it would all be all right in
the end.

The night before we had arranged to go
and collect Honey, April came home early
for tea. She always seems to arrive home
early when it's lasagne, even if Mum doesn't

tell her that's what we're
having. I think she's got
special lasagne-radar-
smell-o-vision and smells it
across town before it's even in the oven.

A little something we have
in common!

'A friend of mine knows someone who
works at the new vets' surgery in town,' she
told me.

'I know,' I said. 'You told me
that when we went shopping. And you
mentioned it quite a few several times last
night.'

April seemed to be very keen on getting
Honey registered with this new vet in town.
I had thought her only interest was going to
be in shopping for all manner of dog-type

63

equipment, especially as she is always telling me that she is far too busy at work in her office to do anything other than really important things like go shopping.

'That'll be useful,' said Mum.

'Don't we have a vet already for the cats?' I asked. I admit that I would not necessarily have known this, as I've never really got involved with Cheese or Toast's medical requirements.

'What would you know? You've never got involved with Cheese or Toast's medical requirements,' said Mum.

Cheese and Toast were both sitting at my feet and chose this moment to start purring loudly, as if they agreed with Mum.

I tried to imagine what Honey would have to say . . .

In the end I couldn't think of an Appropriate Response to Mum's cutting and sarcastic remarks and instead I concentrated on getting the crispy edge of the lasagne before April could dive in and hack off her usual unfairly huge share.

'If you really are interested, Summer,' Mum continued, 'the cats have not been to the vet that much.' (Well, no wonder I didn't know about their medical requirements then!) 'They've only been for their booster jabs once a year, but since they last went, the old surgery has closed down. I've been meaning to register them with the new one, but I'm just too busy. And I'm about to get busier with Honey arriving –'

The cats purred even louder. I wondered if they knew who Honey was.

65

Hey, everyone around here knows about me!

I cut in quickly in a tactful manner to stop Mum starting up on an Anti-Puppy Rant. The closer we got to Honey's arrival, the more Mum was getting more stressed and anxious, and I didn't want her to suddenly change her mind about getting Honey.

'If you have the phone number, April, I'll call the vet and make an appointment to register her as soon as possible,' I offered in a very Responsible Dog-Owner way.

April blushed, which I thought at the time was a weird and strange thing to do when discussing registering a puppy with the vet. 'It's OK,' she said. 'I've already done that.'

Mum dropped her knife and fork on to her plate very dramatically and let her jaw

66

drop, which was a bit disgusting as she still had bits of lasagne in her mouth which I could see in detail as I was sitting opposite her. She should listen to her own advice which she always gives to me on a regular basis about keeping my mouth shut while eating.

'I think I'm going to faint!' she said, being even more over-dramatical. 'Could it be? Yes – I think both daughters are actually using their initiative and being *helpful* for the first time in living memory. Actually, I must be dreaming.' And she pinched herself to check whether or not she was really awake.

And she thinks April and I are behaving strangely?

6
How to Welcome Your Puppy

At last it was the half-term holiday and time to get Honey and bring her home to live with ME! Of course I did not sleep an entire wink the whole of the night before the BIG DAY. When I could at last see light peeping through the curtains in my room I got dressed as quietly as a very small mouse and thought I would start the day off with an exceptionally good deed, i.e. Make Breakfast. So I crept downstairs and started to make toast and get the mugs and plates out. I also moved the dog crate which we had finally bought for Honey. I thought it would be more cosier and comfier nearer the window and out of the way of draughts from the back door. I probably didn't do this particular thing as quietly as a very small mouse, because very small mice can't move large dog crates.

'What on earth are you doing, Summer?' It was Mum, looking, if I may say, quite unglamorous and disorganized, considering what an important day it was for us all.

'I'm making a special breakfast and tidying up the kitchen!' I announced proudly.

'It's half past six,

Summer, on a Saturday morning!' Mum wailed in a WOEBEGONE fashion. (I like the word 'woebegone'. Molly told me it means 'suffering or unhappy', which is exactly how Mum looked at this moment in time.)

'Well, Frank said we could come early, and I know Molly will be up bright-eyed and bushy-tailed – or maybe I'm getting her confused with Honey, ho ho!' I tried Joking to De-Fuse the Tension again. I don't think I'm all that good at it.

You might have a point there.

Mum groaned loudly and stomped back upstairs to bed.

Oh well, more toast for me, I thought, and went to watch a recording of an episode of *Seeing Stars* (which I had missed due to having to do homework or something else equally dull and unimportant) while Mum had a bit of a lie-in. I didn't seem to have woken April, but then, as Mum says, 'April wouldn't get up early on a Saturday morning even if Jude Law was waiting outside to take her on a date,' which is obviously a ridiculous thing to say, as a famous actor like Jude Law is hardly likely to take any interest whatsoever in my grumpy sister when he has got a whole range of Hollywood celebrity babes to choose from to go on a date with. And anyway, if he was waiting outside, April *would* be out of bed and downstairs faster than it takes to blink very quickly, so Mum is just altogether wrong.

We *finally* got to Frank's to find Molly waiting for us. Mum looked a bit better now. She'd made an effort to put on some make-up, which I think made her look a little less tired-looking, but I noticed her socks were odd colours. One was blue and one was red. I tried not to look at them again in case I drew anyone else's attention to them. It would have been far too embarrassing. At least she wasn't wearing her fluffy slippers, thank goodness. She did once forget to take them off when she drove me to school one morning when we were late, and all my friends saw her and I nearly died right there on the spot. Luckily I think everyone was too excitable about the puppies this morning to notice odd socks.

We'd brought the car round to get Honey, even though Frank's house is only a few streets away. We didn't want to carry her all the way home in case she was wriggly and I dropped her.

On the way home I held her on my lap and she made loads of whiny noises that made me feel sad.

What do you expect? You smell weird, and the NOISE...

Frank had warned me about this.

'She will probably cry a bit, tonight especially,' he had said, 'but you must be firm with her.'

'What do you mean?' I asked. When Mum is firm with me I don't get any pocket money for a week, and I certainly am not allowed to watch *Seeing Stars*.

'I mean,' said Frank, in a voice which he probably thought was patient, but which was actually quite rude, 'that you mustn't go and see her in the night if she cries. You must leave her and then she'll learn to be OK on her own. That's what we did with Meatball.'

(I would cry all night if I'd been christened 'Meatball'.)

Mum looked more than a little bit concerned at this point. 'How loudly will she cry?' she asked, crumpling her forehead in a worried way.

Mrs Gritter smiled and said, 'All I can say is, buy yourselves some earplugs just in case.'

I thought that it would be a good idea to leave at this point, in case Frank or Mrs Gritter said anything else completely insensitively that might put Mum off letting me take Honey home. Luckily Honey was still looking very cute and cuddly and so Mum's face went all soft and gooey again when she looked at her.

74

I can't help it – Cute's my middle name!

When we got to my house Molly got out of the car first, and I passed Honey to her as I didn't want to drop her while I climbed out.

Frank had also given us some tiny brown dog-biscuity food that we had to feed to Honey three times a day. I went and put it on a shelf in the kitchen.

'What do we do now?' Mum asked.

April was hopping from foot to foot in a quite impatient and strange way. I thought maybe she needed to go for a pee. That reminded me of the very important thing I had learned from the *Love Me, Love My Dog* book about what to do when the puppy first comes home.

'We have to show Honey where she's allowed to go to the loo,' I said, feeling very important and responsible. 'I shall take her down to the bottom of the garden.'

I carried the warm, snuffly bundle, which was MY WISH COME TRUE, down the garden to our apple tree and said, feeling very proud and bubbly and almost like I might cry all at the same time, 'Empty!' This is the command that Monica Sitstill says you must use to tell your dog when to go to the loo.

Honey just sat there looking extremely small and tiny, like a little golden bear. She put her head on one side like she was really trying to understand me, but it was quite obvious that no one had told her what the word 'Empty' meant.

Sorry, no idea what you're on about.

I sighed and picked her up again and carried her into the kitchen. I put her down on the floor while I made sure that her dog crate was nice and cosily comfy. I was just gently and lovingly arranging her toys and blanket when Mum screamed.

It seemed Honey had finally worked out what 'Empty' meant.

'Argh! Summer, I thought you'd just taken her outside to do a pee!' Mum shrieked as a puddle spread over the kitchen floor.

How most irritating, I thought, as I stood and watched the wetness run down the line in between the kitchen tiles.

Hey, the lady seems excited about something.

'Don't just stand there!' Mum bellowed. 'Get a cloth, get a mop, get some paper towels!'

What an over-the-top PALAVER, as Molly says when everything is a mess and a bother.

I first of all took Honey and put her out in the garden again. Everyone knows (especially if you have read the excellent and informative book *Love Me, Love My Dog*) that you don't scream at a small new puppy who has just done a pee. In the book Monica Sitstill says, 'Praise the good behaviour and ignore the bad.' I think this is a glorious and marvellous way of bringing up animals *and* children to be Model Citizens and I only wish that Mum would make that her personal MOTTO

when it comes to me too. If she ignored
me when I got a bad report, I'm sure I
wouldn't get one again, and especially
I wouldn't if she praised me when I *didn't*
get a bad report!

When I had cleared up the mess in the
kitchen in a very efficient and effective
manner I went back to the garden to get
Honey and take her to her crate. She had
fallen asleep on the patio. My heart grew
at least three sizes in
my chest (as they
say in books) as I
looked on MY WISH
COME TRUE.

19

Puppy Love

I scooped her up into my arms and put her gently into her new bed.

'Welcome to your new home, Honey Love!' I whispered.

7
How to Behave
at the Vets'

By now Honey had spent a whole entire week at our house and had managed to stop crying at night *and* stop peeing on the floor every hour of every day. And I had spent the whole entire week (because it was half-term, so I didn't have to go to school – thank the high heavens for that) staring at Honey while she was sleeping, playing with Honey while she was awake, and staring at Honey while she was feeding. I was OVER THE TOP OF

81

THE MOON and HEAD OVER HEELS in love, which generally meant I felt quite GIDDY most of the time.

One thing I was certainly not feeling giddy about though was that we had to take Honey to the vet for her injections. In fact, I was Exceedingly Worried and Stressed about the injections, as I cannot say I particularly like the sight of a needle when it is going to be used for an injection, even if it is *not* going to be used to inject *me*. But April was being so kind and helpful and said she would come with me and hold my hand and Honey's paw if necessary. All very strange and UNCHARACTERISTIC.

'Haven't you got lots of exceedingly important work in your office?' I asked.

'Oh well, that can wait,' said my sister in an airy, careless sort of way. She kept

checking her reflection in the hall mirror
and turning her head
to one side and the
other and patting
her long blonde
hair. I have
always wished
so much that
I had my sister's long blonde hair. Not
actually her own hair, obviously, because
then that would make my sister bald, and
I'm not such a meany as all that. But it
would be nice to wake up one day and
have magically changed into a girl with
long blonde hair instead of being me with
short, curly auburn hair.

You know what they say:
We Blondes have all the fun!

'Why are you checking your hair so much?'
I asked. 'We are only going to the vet.'

April frowned at me and then tutted
as if to say, 'Honestly, you don't know
anything about what it is to be a girl with
long blonde hair.' But she didn't actually
say anything, just grabbed Honey from
me and put her in the boot of Mum's car
and told me to get in too. (Not in the
boot, of course.)

When we got to the vet we were
actually quite early. I thought this was
strange, as April never manages to be early
for anything. In fact, Mum says, 'April
Lydia Love, you'll be late for your own
funeral,' which I think is a daft thing to
say, as how can you be late when you are
already dead?

The new vets' surgery was a very smart
building and had one entrance for people

with dogs and one for people with small pets like cats and hamsters and stick insects and things. Actually, I wonder if people really do take stick insects to the vet ever? I never did take mine. But they escaped from their jar after only two weeks of owning them, so I didn't really get the chance. Mum doesn't know they escaped. She would obviously FREAK if she knew, in case they might be living under her bed or something, which of course they might be . . .

The dog side of the building was a crazy and noisy place to be. The waiting room was full of dogs, barking and whining and trying to play with each other.

What a racket . . .
some of us are trying to
snooze, you know.

Puppy Love

Luckily for us, Honey was small enough to sit on our laps and be held and she was actually quite sleepy, as she always was when we first had her. I was thinking about the old saying that people look like their dogs — or is it that dogs look like their owners? — and playing a game of looking around and trying to see if it was true. And the people DID look like their dogs. There was a scary kind of droopy-mouthed dog which I think is what you call a bulldog. He was snarling a lot and had gloops of sticky stuff hanging from his jaws.

Someone needs to go to the pooch parlour, methinks.

It was quite the most disgustingest kind of beast, and I was ever so thoroughly glad that Honey did not look like that.

Thank You so much!

Then I looked up and saw
that the man who was holding on to the
scary beast's lead was also very scary-
looking! And he had a droopy kind of face
with dribbly, gloopy bits coming out of his
mouth too. I had to look away and pretend
to examine my chewcd-off nails to hide my
laughter. I didn't want the scary man and
dog to jump on me or dribble on me or
anything.

And then I looked up and saw a very
skinny dog with very short, grey silvery hair
and long dangly ears. I think it must have
been a she-dog because it was wearing a
very glistening and glimmering collar with
what I'm sure were real diamonds on it.
The famous people in the magazines Molly
brings to our Celebrity Club meetings all

87

have dogs with very real diamond collars
on. I wondered how much an actual real
diamond collar would cost and whether I
could maybe try to get on *Seeing Stars* and
become famous and get loads of money and
buy one for Honey.

I wouldn't say no . . .

Then I looked up and saw that dog's owner
and started feeling like I was going to laugh
all over again, because that owner was
another person who looked exactly spot-on
like her dog! The woman had long grey
hair that looked like her dog's ears and she
was even wearing an actual real diamond
necklace, which is called a choker because
it looks like it's so tight round your neck it
will actually really choke you. This time my
laughter was really getting far too difficult

and frankly uncomfortable to control and I
burst out with a laugh just as the vet came
out and called:

'Puppy Love – please come through!'

This sounded quite bizarre of course to
everyone in the room, and they all laughed
because there is an expression 'puppy love',
which means that two very young people
have fallen in love (I read it in one of
Molly's magazines). Even though I was a
bit embarrassed, I was relieved that I could
let my own laughter out quite loudly now
that everyone else was laughing. I thought
this was quite clever of me. April obviously
did not think this and grabbed me tightly by
the hand, hissing, 'Shut up, Summer.'

Why on earth should I have shut up
when everyone else was laughing? I can't
have made April embarrassed if everyone
else was laughing too. And anyway,

she was using very strange and peculiar behaviour, patting her hair, snatching Honey from me and grinning at the vet in a weird daydreamy-ish way.

We went into the vet's room and April stroked Honey and put her on the table.

'Now, what can we do for your lovely new puppy, Ms Love?' asked the vet, looking straight at my sister when he was talking.

'Excuse me,' I said most politely. I wanted to correct his obvious mistake about the important fact that Honey was indeed MY lovely new puppy.

Yeah, excuse me too! First you get my name wrong, then you ignore me and talk to the girl!

'Yes, she is lovely, isn't she?' said my sister.

I thought it was very rude of her to butt in and ignore me. But I didn't say anything because I was distracted by the tone of her voice, which was all sugary and yucky-sounding and so I found myself staring at her instead. She flicked her blonde hair over her shoulders and I started dreaming again about having nice hair and thinking, 'I wish I could do that,' so I missed what the vet said back to her.

Then I looked hard at the vet and wondered how old he was. Maybe about the same age as April, sort of twenties-ish. He had nice sparkly blue eyes and a very friendly smile and a little short beard. I wish men didn't have beards. It makes it so difficult to work out how old they are, and of course it is very bad manners indeed to *ask* them how old they are, so you just

have to guess. Then I thought, 'How do
you eat when you have a beard? Does food
get stuck in it? I wouldn't like to kiss a man
with a beard. It would be so prickly, I am
sure of that. But then, maybe beard-hair is
soft like a puppy's? Urgh! I don't know why
I thought that. *I don't like kissing*, beard or
no beard!'

I suddenly realized that Honey was not
happy at all. She was pulling away from
the vet and whimpering.

ARGH! Have you seen the
man's face? Freak out!

I snapped myself out of my dreaming and
tried to calm Honey down. (It was actually
a relief to be able to stop thinking about
kissing men with beards.) April was holding
Honey down on to the table tightly with

93

one hand and trying to ignore how much
she was wriggling and whining, while she
flicked her blonde hair around with her
other hand and chatted away in that
yucky voice.

'Yes, I work for Quincey and Close on
the High Street,' she was saying.

Aha! So they're not actually called
Stingy and Gross . . .

But it wasn't really the moment to
check with April what her place of work
was really called as Honey was starting
to yowl and was looking at Mr Beard
in a very scared manner and trying to
back away from him off the table. I
think she had worked out about the
injection.

Forget the needle — look at
the face! Don't you think
it's weird?

I glowered in a way that I thought told my
sister to stop chatting and to let poor Honey
get her major ordeal of being injected
over and done with. April did not see the
glowering, so I put my own hand on Honey

95

and pinched my sister's hand to get her to move it from MY puppy.

'Ouch! Summer, what are you doing – *sweetie?*' said April, rubbing her hand and pretending to still smile at me while actually gritting her teeth in a threatening way.

'Sweetie?' I repeated, feeling quite baffled as she never ever calls me that. But I couldn't say any more, because Honey squirmed round and nipped *me* on the hand and then fell off the table in a howling heap.

 Hairy Face stabbed me!

'There, all done,' said Mr Beard.

I did not know what he meant, but then I saw he was holding a syringe in his hand – he was holding it up in the air in his rubber-gloved hand just like they do on the telly in those doctor programmes and I thought, Thank goodness, he must have done the injection when I wasn't looking.

And then I fainted.

8
How to Behave at a Puppy Party

April was strangely cross with me after the fainting episode at the vets', which I thought was very Hurtful and Uncaring and even Unsisterly of her. I said so, but she just said that I was the Unsisterly one and that I should know better than to embarrass her by pinching her and fainting in public.

Mum laughed far too long and loud when I told her about the visit to the vet and about how April had chatted annoyingly to Mr Beard and not let me say anything about MY puppy. I didn't see one little bit what was so funny, especially since the whole visit had been a Major Ordeal for me and for poor little Honey.

You said it, sister.

Apparently I'd missed out on the best bit while I'd been lying on the floor in my dramatical fainting fit, because Mr Beard had invited me, April and Honey to a 'puppy party' the next week! It had to be in the evening so that people could get there after work. This was something April was apparently very pleased about. I was pleased too, as I was of course at school in the day.

'I love parties!' I cried, immediately feeling a bit better, even though I did have an impressive lump on my head which I kept on rubbing as I wanted Mum and April to see that I still needed lots of Tea and Sympathy. (Although I actually prefer hot chocolate and marshmallows.)

'Can Molly come? Can we dress up? Do we get to eat cake and play Pass the Parcel?' I blushed when I said that last bit, as everyone knows Pass the Parcel is a very babyish-type game, but I love it, especially when there is a jelly baby between each layer of the paper.

April did her rolly-eyed sophisticated sighing thing and said, 'No, Summer, we won't be playing silly party games. It's a party for the *puppies*, not for us. And yes, bring your little friend. It might stop you from pinching people and fainting again.'

How to Behave at a Puppy Party

I did not dignify my annoying older
sister with a response to her hurtful and
unsisterly comment, but rushed instead to
call Molly and ask her if she wanted to
come to the puppy party.

'Does the sun rise in the morning?'
she asked.

So we started planning what we were
going to wear (which obviously takes a
week's worth of planning) and whether or
not we should bring our cameras in case
there were any celebrity dog owners there
or maybe even teacherly Monica Sitstill,
telly personality and dog trainer *extraordinaire*
(that's French for fab, according to Molly
who is as good at French as she is at, well,
everything really).

In the end the puppy party was quite good
fun, but unfortunately as it was at the

vets' and not at a glam Venue of any sort,
there were no celebrities, just Mr Beard —
although you would have thought he was a
celebrity the way April spent the whole time
fluttering her eyelashes and flicking her hair
and crossing and uncrossing her legs. She
was obviously pleased to see him again.

Honey was not.

Hey! He's hairy and he
hurts puppies! Who would be
pleased to see HIM?

She took one look at him when we arrived
at the party and whined and hid her head
in my jacket.

Molly nudged me and pointed at my
sister and said, 'Do you think April's all
right? She looks as if she is desperate for the
loo all the time. Do you think I should tell

her that there's one out in reception?'

I just said, 'No, let's concentrate on Honey.'

So we did.

Once Mr Beard had moved away from us to talk to some other people, Honey calmed down a bit and ended up having a marvellously fabulous time at the party. Apparently the whole idea about a puppy party is to get the dogs to Socialize and Interact. I worked out that this means 'get used to other dogs'. Honey is not a shy dog, I have found.

I like to Work the room, you know?

She spotted the biggest dog there, which unfortunately was the huge slobbery dog with the dribble that I'd seen in the vets'

waiting room when we came for the
injections, and she ran over and put her
paws around his neck.

I'm not Backward in
coming forward!

The big slobbery owner with the scary
droopy face just stared at Honey. I tried
to engage him in some polite chatty
conversation about how nice it was to see
our puppies playing together. It's the kind of
thing I've heard Mum say to another mum
when I make a new friend and go round
to their house. But the scary slobbery man
had obviously not mastered the art of polite
chatty conversation himself, because he just
stared at me like he had stared at Honey.
Then his dog growled at Honey and tried
to bite her.

So you like to play rough, do you?

I wanted to get her back, but Mr Beard piped up at this point and said, 'Don't worry, Autumn, that's just natural dog behaviour.'

'I'm called Summer,' I said sternly, 'and I don't like the way that dog growled at my puppy—'

'Ahem, what my little sister means is that I'm sometimes a bit overprotective of my dog,' said April, cutting in and ASTOUNDING me with her lying, which would be described as Bare-Faced, I think. In other words – OUTRAGEOUS!

'Sorry – Summer – and er . . . ?' Mr Beard looked questioningly at April, which seemed to make her face go a sort of dark red unattractively sweaty kind of colour,

and she said, 'A–April,' and giggled. I
was still very upset by the way she was
pretending that Honey was *her* dog, so I
couldn't find the words to say anything at
all at this point, but it didn't matter as Mr
Beard was still wittering on.

'Don't worry about the growling. It's
only a little warning so that Honey doesn't
get too big for her boots and play too
roughly,' he said.

Molly and I exchanged a look when he
said this. I knew she was thinking the same
thing as me (we quite often do): how could
Honey be too rough for such a horrible
huge slobbery monster? I was about to say
something, but Honey was actually quite
happily rolling around with Slobberchops
again, and anyway, Mr Beard wanted to
tell us about a game called Pass the Puppy.

Aha! I thought. No 'silly party games',

eh, April? and I tried to smirk knowingly at my sister to show her that I'd been right all along, as indeed I often am.

But April was looking rather stressed and was furiously wiping at her white jeans in a quite panicky manner. Honey had bounded up to her after finishing her game with Slobberchops and had nuzzled her cute little pink nose all over April's jeans.

Just Being friendly!

Normally puppy-nuzzling is something lovely; it was just a shame that Honey had got herself totally covered in Slobberchops's slobber and was now getting April's white jeans covered in it too.

We played Pass the Puppy. (Well, Molly and I did. April didn't bother to join in as she was being what Mum calls

a Prima Donna and fussing over her jeans
and smoothing down her long blonde hair,
while she and Mr Beard nattered on about
something dull.) The game was basically
just the owners passing their puppy on to
the owner next to them, so that we all got
a chance to make a fuss of different puppies.
The puppies were supposed to get used to
being handled by different types of people.
The only thing was, the puppies were more
interested in the other puppies than in their

boring owners, so we didn't get much of chance to pat and cuddle them.

Newsflash — dogs are more interesting than people!

So we all gave up quite quickly and just let them roll around on the floor and chew each other's ears and sniff each other's bottoms which is what puppies seem to like doing more than anything.

What else is there in life?

Then at the end of the party, when the puppies were all quite worn out and exhausted, Mr Beard actually stopped talking to my sister for about five minutes and told us all about pet insurance. This was possibly the most BORING thing I have ever had to sit through in my whole long life; even more dull and deadly boring than the Victorians and their completely useless penny-farthing-type inventions.

So I started whispering with Molly about the latest programme of *Seeing Stars*, which I'd seen the night before. There had been this really lame act on which was a man who thought

he was so cool because he could ride on
a bicycle with only one wheel (which is
called a Monocle, I think) while balancing
a plate of sausages on his head and singing
'Is This the Way to Amarillo?', and he was
wearing a purple shiny suit, so honestly how
on earth he could have possibly thought he
was cool is beyond me. Also, he sang out of
tune. Also, why on earth would you want
to balance sausages? Surely he could have
come up with something more glam than
that? Of course, he didn't get many points.
And the judges were so rude! They said
to him that they would gladly show him
the way to Amarillo if only he'd take his
Monocle and ride off there right away and
take his sausages with him. It had made me
laugh till I needed the loo quite desperately.

Anyway, as I was telling Molly this
hilarious thing, I was holding Honey on

my lap. She'd gone to sleep, and she was being so quiet that I'd unfortunately sort of forgotten she was there, so when I did a marvellous and extremely realistic impression of balancing a plate of sausages on my head while wobbling on a Monocle bike, I accidentally knocked Honey and she fell off my lap at Mr Beard's feet. She woke up at once . . .

Who wouldn't, under the circumstances?

. . . and looked up to see Mr Beard bending over her to see if she was all right. Well, one look at him and Honey leaped into the air, yowling and howling and then scarpered back underneath my seat.

Hairy Needle-Man Alert!

How to Behave at a Puppy Party

This had the unfortunate effect of setting
all the other puppies off barking and
howling and they all made a dive for my
seat as well. I think they thought it was
a new party game where they had to
chase Honey.

In the confusion, I was knocked off my
seat and I bashed my head on the shelf
behind me.

And I fainted again.

9

How to Be Ahead of the Game

Mum laughed even longer and louder when I told her about how Honey had reacted to seeing Mr Beard again. Personally I thought she could have been more sensitive and caring about me Losing My Conscienceness, which is what the nurse at the vet's said my fainting had been.

'Looks like April's got a tough job on her hands,' Mum said. I thought this was a cryptical thing to say, and also frankly

a stupid one — as it was *me* that got
knocked out by my puppy being frightened
of Mr Beard, so what did that have to
do with April?

That weekend Molly came round to
my house as usual. Mum and April were
clattering about the kitchen and arguing
about something, so we made ourselves a
snack and played with Honey in what Mum
still calls the Playroom, but which I call the
Den, as it sounds less babyish.

While we were playing, I told Molly
about this cryptical comment of Mum's,
and she said she thought she had worked it
out because, while I was being helped by
the other vets and nurses after my second
faint, Molly was watching my sister and Mr
Beard talking. She secretly spied on them
while pretending to put all her attention on
to Honey.

Yeah, I noticed that.

Molly is very good at secretly spying on people while pretending to put all her attention on to other things. She does it at school all the time. That is how she always manages to Stay Ahead of the Game and know who is best friends with who, and

which parties everyone is going to. This
is why she will make a fabulous famous
journalist when she grows up so that she
can report on all the celebrities we will
meet when we get on the telly with our
Celebrity Club.

'I have worked out all the answers to
the mysteriousness of your sister's recent
behaviour patterns,' Molly told me in a
hushed and secretive way.

'Eh?' I said.

'I know why your sister's being weird,'
Molly explained, sighing in an annoying
Mum-type manner.

'Oh good,' I said. 'Does it have
anything to do with Honey? Because I am
feeling rather confused and upset about her
pretending Honey is *her* puppy.'

Molly smirked in a way that made
me realize she absolutely *did* have all the

117

answers and was dying to let me know how clever she was. 'Well, you're on the right lines,' she said.

'Molly, just tell me,' I said in a grumpy tone. 'I am not in a mood to play guessing games of any sort.'

'It's all to do with Mr Beard!' she cried triumphantly. 'Except that is not his real name.'

'I know that!' I shouted. Then I realized I didn't actually know what his real name was. 'What is his real name then?' I asked more quietly.

> Mr Beard
> *Veterinary*
> *Surgeon*

'It's Nick Harris,' she said smugly.

'What a boring and dull grown-up name,' I said. I was disappointed. Mr Beard was actually a much better and more DESCRIPTIVE name.

'Well, I can't do anything about that,' said Molly. She was starting to seriously

annoy me now. She might be my best
friend, but she can still wind me up when
she wants to. Or even sometimes when she
doesn't want to. 'He's called Nick Harris
and he's only just become a vet because he's
been a student until now, which means he's
not that much older than your sister,' said
Molly, still smirking.

This was not exactly an exciting piece of
news that could be called a REVELATION
at all.

I put on a mega-sulk, which involved
me crossing my arms, rolling my eyes and
saying, 'So?' in a huffy way.

'*So?*' Molly cried. '*So*, it's a very
important bit of information which makes
everything else fit into the picture perfectly.'

Molly was being as cryptical as Mum,
and I was distinctively losing interest in this
conversation. I turned to walk away, and

Molly realized how much I was distinctively
losing interest in this conversation, so she
quickly said, 'April's in love with him.'

'Argh!' I screamed. I couldn't help it.
April was IN LOVE WITH HIM? This
meant my sister was going to KISS A
MAN WITH A BEARD!

My scream frightened Honey, who
had been following me as I was about
to leave the room. She jumped back and
yelped.

So would you if someone trod
on your tail.

Molly put her hand on my arm to calm me
down. 'It's OK. I don't think *he* is in love
with *her*,' she said quickly.

'Phew!' I said.

'Yet,' she said.

'What do you mean, 'yet'?' I asked.

'The thing is, Mr Be— I mean, Nick Harris, thinks Honey is April's dog doesn't he?' said Molly.

'Yes,' I said, 'and I'm very cross about—'

'I know,' said Molly, 'but listen. Nick thinks that Honey is April's new pride and joy, and it's quite obvious that Honey does not like Nick Harris, because both times she's seen him Honey has gone mad and barked and howled like a crazy thing.'

Who you calling crazy?

I thought this was quite a harsh and unkind and unsupportive thing to say about my new puppy, and was going to say so, but Molly didn't give me a chance.

Puppy Love

'I was listening to Nick Harris and April talking, and April was saying, "Wouldn't it be lovely to go for a walk with Honey together? I would so much appreciate your professional opinion on training her," and Nick Harris said, "That would be so lovely indeed, but I don't think your dog likes me very much." And your sister kept trying other ways of saying how nice it would be to meet and Nick Harris kept talking to her in an extremely friendly way, but saying that he didn't think it would be a good idea to upset Honey while she was still so small. So he obviously does not want to go out with April, so I don't think he's in love with her *yet*.'

'Well, that's that then,' I said, feeling not a small bit relieved that Mr Beard wouldn't be going out with my sister all the time. And maybe KISSING her. Urgh!

Molly was looking worried. 'I'm afraid that's not,' she said.

'That's not what?' I said, confused and bewildered.

'That's not that, I'm afraid,' she said. 'You see, if you go into the kitchen, you will find your sister sitting reading *Love Me, Love My Dog* and discussing with your mum about how to DESENSITIZE Honey to Men With Beards.'

'*What?*' I cried. 'I thought they were arguing about April running riot with Mum's credit card again.'

'They were, but they've moved on from that,' Molly said, sounding smug again. 'When I went to the loo just now I hovered invisibly by the kitchen door and listened to what they were saying. This is what journalists have to do at parties and things to get juicy Celebrity Gossip. And have

I got some juicy gossip for you, Summer
Holly Love!'

'Yeah, yeah,' I said feeling irritated that
I had not thought of this invisible hovering-
in-doorways idea. 'So?'

'*So*, I heard all about how April had
seen Nick Harris in town when you first got
Honey and how she liked him and found
out he worked in the new vets' surgery.
That's why she registered Honey there in
the first place.' said Molly, Warming to
Her Theme. 'And it would now appear
that April is very determined to get Nick
Harris to go out with her – and you know
that when April is very determined, she gets
what she wants.'

'Yes,' I said quietly. 'But how can she
make Nick Harris go out with her if he
doesn't want to?' I asked. Surely not even my
sister has those sorts of powers? I thought.

Molly sighed as if I had overlooked a most obvious and basic thing. 'I heard April say to your mum that the only reason that Honey does not like Nick Harris is because he has a beard, because April has read in our book that puppies who have never seen a man with a beard before often are very scared indeed when they see such a man for the first time. And she has found in the book what she thinks is a Sensible Solution.'

'Good,' I said, thinking the book would say, 'If you care for your puppy's mental sanity, never go near men with beards ever again.'

That's my plan.

'Not good, actually,' said Molly. 'She's decided that she has to get Honey used to beards, because she *needs* Honey so that she can go and see Nick Harris again. She thinks the only way she's going to get Nick Harris to go on a date with her is if it has something to do with Honey, because that's how they met each other in the first place.'

'And how in all the earth is she planning to get Honey used to men with beards? I suppose with all your clever hovering and being invisible and everything, you will have heard that part of the conversation too!' I said grumpily.

'I did,' said Molly. 'You're not going to like this.'

'Tell me,' I demanded fiercely.

'She's going to do what Monica Sitstill advises in the book. She is going to buy some false beards and get us all to wear them.'

ME, WEAR A BEARD?

I nearly almost fainted again.

10
How to Fight Like Cat and Dog

Luckily the beard-buying trip idea was not mentioned when Mum and April came out to say goodbye to Molly when it was time for her to go home. I decided that I did not want to hang around the house in case April *did* mention a beard-buying trip, so I went out into the garden to play with Honey. At least she was sane and normal. Or so I thought.

Actually Honey started doing something really strange with Cheese and Toast. She was creeping towards them on her belly and twitching her head to one side. I thought at first maybe she was ill. I had never seen her move like that before. Cheese and Toast were sitting staring at her, and you could tell they were also thinking this was strange. They were most probably thinking, 'Who is this bizarre creature?'

Who are you calling BiZarre?

How to Fight Like Cat and Dog

Cats always look as if they are thinking this, whoever they are looking at. This is because cats think everyone except another cat is a weird creature. They are HAUGHTY and ALOOF – that's what Molly's mum, Mrs Cook, says. Mrs Cook does not like cats.

Honey then jumped towards Cheese and Toast, and of course they hissed at her and scratched her. They are always hissing and scratching. They even hiss and scratch at *each other*. They used to be good friends when they were kittens, but now they ignore each other or fight. I suppose that's what sisters do in real true human life, so why should cats be any different? Anyway, Honey was frankly very upset by this behaviour. In fact she yelped, as Cheese and Toast have very sharp claws.

Not very friendly, these puppies . . .

But whereas I would most definitely never go near Cheese and Toast again if they scratched me, Honey crept nearer them on her belly again.

These puppies are funny little guys. Why won't they play?

Cheese and Toast looked really very miffed that Honey was not getting their message, and so Cheese pounced on Honey. Honey did not get this message either; she seemed to think it was a message that said, 'Let's play,' but in cat language it of course meant the total opposite of that.

I've told them I'm a nice friendly pooch, But they are just not on my wavelength...

So Honey got scratched again. I decided I should call Mum to come outside as I was getting a bit anxious that Honey might get really hurt, and of course I was not really in the mood for taking her to the vet if she got injured, because I didn't want to see Mr Be– Harris again.

'Mum! Come and see what's going on with Honey and Cheese and Toast!' I shouted.

Mum came out. 'What's the matter?' she asked.

'I'm worried Honey's going to get hurt,' I explained worriedly. 'What can I do? Cheese and Toast keep scratching at her to get her to keep away from them, but Honey

131

keeps trying to get closer to them. It doesn't make any kind of sense. She is basically not getting their message.'

Mum watched the three animals rolling around and crouching and pouncing and then burst out laughing.

'Honey, you daft mutt!' she cried.

Who me?

Honey had stopped rolling around with the cats for a moments and was looking up at me with her head on one side – what if she understood?

'Look, Summer,' said Mum, 'Cheese and Toast speak a completely different language from Honey.'

It would seem so.

I did not understand this. Animals do not speak. Unless maybe my mum had hidden talents like Doctor Dolittle and she could speak to the animals? I was pondering over this particularly strange idea when I realized Mum was still talking to me – in human language.

'The cats lie flat when they are going to pounce and attack something – you've seen them do that when they are trying to catch a bird, haven't you?'

'Yes – so what?'

'Well, when Honey lies flat she's trying to tell the cats that she won't hurt them, she's just being friendly. It's called being submissive,' Mum explained.

That's right. But these little puppies just don't get it!

133

Puppy Love

'I doubt Honey even realizes that Cheese and Toast are cats,' Mum continued. 'Frank didn't have any cats at his house, did he?' I shook my head. 'She probably thinks Cheese and Toast are puppies like her, and she's trying to work out how to play with them. I've been reading your *Love Me, Love My Dog* book with April – there's loads of interesting stuff in there about how new puppies relate to pets that are already in the family,' said Mum.

Yeah, I thought, there's loads of interesting stuff in there about how new puppies relate to beards too. But I didn't say anything as I was trying hard not to think about my sister kissing beardy guys, and anyway, Mum was sounding very pleased with her knowledgableness on the subject of puppies for the first time since we had got Honey, so I didn't want to interrupt.

'I think the only thing we can do about Cheese and Toast is let them sort things out with Honey in their own way. She'll get the message eventually.'

I nodded, but secretly did not think this was a very likely thing, as I watched Honey trying to shake both cats off her back while they held on like their claws were superglued into her fur.

I am beginning to get seriously worried that Mum might in fact be right and that my dog might be one dog biscuit short of a full barrel – in other words, daft.

DAFT? ME? Humph

11
How to Desensitize Your Puppy

My sister, April Lydia Love, had just INSULTED me.

'You and your little friend have been spying on me!' she was yelling. It was not an attractive way to behave, I thought, as it made her face go a tomatoey-ketchupy kind of colour.

'What do you actually mean by

136

"spying"?' I said in a cool and calm way.
(I was doing what Molly calls PLAYING
FOR TIME, which is when you know
you've been caught out, but you don't
want to have to admit it straight away as
you are hoping there might be a way out
of the Difficult Situation you have found
yourself in.)

'YOU KNOW WHAT "SPYING"
MEANS!' shrieked April in a scarily
dramatical manner, flicking her hair
around quite fiercesomely and huffing
like a steam train.

If only Nick could see you now, I
thought, a little bit meanly.

'I HEARD MOLLY TELL YOU
ABOUT ME FANCYING NICK
AND ABOUT HIS BEARD AND
EVERYTHING!' April was really quite
shouting by this point.

137

'Oh,' I said.

That was all I could manage to say. I was actually suddenly speechless with shock that my only sister could stoop so incredibly low as to spy on me and my best friend having a private conversation. (Even though I suppose Molly *had* been spying on *her* before. But then, April is older than us and really should know better.)

'So, *Summer*,' April said, in less of a shouty way (more of an 'I'm your older sister, so you'd better listen up' tone of speaking), 'the cat really is out of the bag now. And to make it up to me, you and your little friend are going to come shopping with me for beards.'

'WHAT?' I almost nearly choked to death right there on the very spot. 'You want us to go and buy a false beard together – and you've been keeping the cats in a bag as *well*?' I wailed at my sister. How much more mad could a person get? If this was what love did to you, I for one was NEVER going to fall in it . . .

'Are you really that stupid, or do you just enjoy winding me up?' April asked.

I didn't think I would dignify that extremely rude and unnecessary question with a grown-up response.

I rang Molly and asked her if she would come with me for this humiliating experience. Of course she said yes, but I didn't think it was because she wanted to support me. Secretly I thought she was doing it to get a bit of a laugh and to collect valuable material for future articles she would write about her childhood life when she was eventually famous. Or maybe she wasn't interested in becoming famous any more. We had not had much time to do our Celebrity Club recently, what with all the puppy stuff and spying on my sister and now going on a shopping trip for beards.

April drove us into town in Mum's car as I said I absolutely did not want to be seen walking back from town carrying a bag of beards and that we would have to put them in the boot. April did at least see the sensibleness of this suggestion.

We went to a shop called Dressed to Thrill. It was advertised as a theatrical supplies shop, but actually in true life it was more of a fancy-dress shop, where everyone went when they wanted to get an outfit for a party or a school show or something. It was not really a proper theatrical sort of place where celebrities go. The costumes were all shiny and quite unreal and didn't look at all how proper nurses/queens/

firemen/Robin Hoods would dress. It was
never very convincing when you got a
costume from there. I knew this because I
had to go there with Mum for parties and
things. I never really felt In Character like
a real actor would when I was dressed in
something from there. Once I went to a
party dressed as Cinderella and the rags
from the dress kept falling off and I had to
stick them back on again with bits
of chewing gum as that was
all I had with me at the time.

   I think if you were in a play
and you wanted to look like a true-life
King Henry the Eighth, for example, you
would have to write to the BBC and ask
them for a costume, because they are the
only ones who really know what a true-life
King Henry the Eighth would look like. He
most certainly would not wear shiny clothes

made from nylon and plastic, which is all
you get from Dressed to Thrill. I don't even
know why it's called Dressed to Thrill, as I
have never been thrilled in any way about
anything I have ever seen in there.

So you can see why I was not at all
sure that we would even find a beard in the
shop that would look like a true-life beard.
In fact, I was quite hopeful we would not.

In any case, the man who ran the shop
was 'the looniest of loony tunes on Radio
Loony', to quote Molly, and I was not
looking forward to having to talk to him.

'Hello, luvvies!' he cried as soon
as we entered his totally dodgy
ESTABLISHMENT. The bell on the door
played the first few bars of one of the songs
from Disney's *Beauty and the Beast*, which I
found very annoying and showy-offy, and
actually somewhat childish.

'Now, luvvies, what are we after today?' the man asked. He was dressed in an OUTLANDISH and frankly embarrassing-to-look-at outfit of a piratical nature. He had a huge white blouse instead of a normal man's shirt and wore those big pirate-ish boots over black trousers. And he had a twirly black moustache, which I know wasn't real as it wasn't on straight. It didn't bode well for the beards.

'Hello,' said April in her businesslike work voice that she uses if ever you call her in the office at Stingy and Gross or whatever it's called. 'We've come to buy some beards.'

143

'Aha! In a lovely play together, are you, luvvies? One of those fabulous Shakespearian ones where the ladies get to dress up as men?' he chortled in an overenthusiastic way, as if he got an immense amount of pleasure from selling beards to people on a daily basis.

'Y-yes,' stammered April. I was shocked that she was doing another one of her Bare-Faced Lies, but then I supposed she couldn't really tell him the truth, which was of course: 'No, we are desensitizing our puppy to men with beards, as I have fallen in love with a vet with a beard but the puppy doesn't like him.'

'*Lovely*, luvvies!' cried the man, and he threw his arms up in the air in a very over-the-top dramatical gesture, which made his moustache detach itself completely on one side and nearly come off. He didn't seem to notice though and swung round to face the rest of the shop, calling out to us to follow him to the Facial Hair section.

We spent the next hour trying on various different colours and shapes and sizes of beard. April was very fussy and critical the whole time and got exceedingly impatient with me and Molly when we had rather a long giggling session. I have found it is honestly very difficult not to have a rather long giggling session while trying on beards.

In the end we did find three small beards that were sort of like the one that Nick Harris had, and we paid for them and put them in a bag and hurried back to the car.

When we got home, April made us put the beards on in the car.

I was very dead set against this. 'I'll

145

put mine on inside,' I said firmly. 'What
if someone from school saw me wearing
a beard? I would never live it down if I
was known at school as the Bearded Lady
or Beardy Weirdy or something cruel and
unkind like that.'

'No,' said April, even more firmly, 'it's
very important that Honey sees us with
the beards as soon as we walk through the
door. We'll just confuse her if we go into
the kitchen looking normal and then put the
beards on in front of her.'

'Heavens above forbid that we should
look *normal*,' muttered Molly in the
sort of tone her mum uses when she is
getting impatient with Molly's dad about
something, which is quite often.

I thought I might start a long giggling
session again, but then I caught the look on
my sister's face – it was a very determined

and angry look — and I thought perhaps
another long giggling session was not a
good idea just at that moment.

We put on our beards and scurried
around to the back entrance of the house
so that no one would see us. We went in

through the kitchen and there was cute little Honey, sitting in her crate, waiting for us to come back. Unfortunately as soon as she saw us she went BANANAS-DOOLALLY-CRAZY, barking like she'd gone totally mad, and started trying to eat her way out of the crate.

Smell's Bells! Who are these hairy guys?

'Quick!' said April. 'Back out again!'

We went back out.

'What are you doing?' I asked. 'I thought you wanted us to go in with our beards on?'

'I do, but we have to keep coming in and going out until she *doesn't* bark when she sees us come in,' said April. Talk about confusing – and to think I'd been worried

about *Honey* getting muddled. 'The minute she sees us with beards and *doesn't* bark, we let her out of the crate and give her a big hug and a treat,'
April continued.

This sounded loop - the *loop* to me.

'It's what it says in *Love Me, Love My Dog*,' said April. 'It says, "Your puppy has to realize that Good Things happen around men with beards."'

Molly sniggered. 'That's what you're hoping, isn't it, April?'

April glowered. At least I think she did. It was a bit difficult to see behind the beard.

So we spent what felt like hours going in and out of the house trying to get Honey used to the beards. Eventually we had to stop because we were all getting hot and

sweaty in our facial hair, and I told April
that I thought Honey needed to get out
of her crate and go to the loo in the
garden.

Forget the loo –
I JUST WANT OUT!

April went off in a huffy mood into the
sitting room, still wearing her beard. Perhaps
wearing it made her feel closer to Nick
Harris, like she was already KISSING HIS
BEARD or something. URGH! She turned
on the telly and flopped crossly down on to
the sofa.

I angrily shoved my beard into the bag
we'd brought it home in and took
poor Honey outside. She immediately
calmed down and jumped up to lick
my face.

Hey, You're Back! You should have seen these hairy guys that kept coming in and out while you were away . . .

'The things you do for love, eh?' said Molly, pulling off her beard as well and following us out to the garden.

'Humph,' I muttered. I was truly miffed and embarrassed by this whole palaver and determined not to do this beard-desensitizing thing ever again. 'What are we going to do, Molly? We have to get April to stop wanting to use Honey to get to Nick Harris. Honey is *my* puppy. Why should April get away with upsetting her like this? I don't care if Honey doesn't like beards! I don't like them either. I wish Mum would tell April to sort out her Romantic Problem on her own and leave me and Honey out of it.'

Molly nodded. Then she laughed.

'Why are you laughing?' I cried in an exasperated tone. 'You are my Best Friend. Best Friends do not laugh in times of crisis like this one. You should be helping me.'

'I know – that's why I laughed. I have had an idea,' she said. 'Listen, what if we put Nick Harris off your sister once and for all so that he absolutely definitely totally does not want to go out with her?'

Now this was possibly quite an unkind thing to do, and probably definitely unsisterly. I thought about it for a split moment and then said, 'OK. What do you have in mind?'

Molly told me her Masterly Plan.

And I laughed too.

12
How to Desensitize
Your Vet

Molly persuaded me to put her
Masterly Plan into operation straight
away while my extremely annoying and
embarrassing older sister was watching telly. I
agreed at once in case I thought about it too
much and decided to change my mind.

Molly used the kitchen phone to ring the
vets' surgery.

'Hello, may I please speak with Mr
Nicholas Harris the vet, please,' she said.
She put on a posh telephone voice which

was extremely EFFECTIVE and made
her sound older and definitely maturer.
'Oh, he's out making house calls?
Actually, would it be possible to contact
him and ask him to make a house
call here to my particular place of abode?'
Molly was possibly slightly overdoing the
posh telephone voice, but I thought she must
know what she was doing. 'Thank you so
much. It's my puppy you see – Honey. Yes,
Honey Love, that's the one. She's ever so
poorly and really I can't see how I would get
her in the car . . . so Mr Harris will be here
shortly? Thank you so much. My name? Yes,
certainly. It's April Love.'

I was quite a little bit SHOCKED by
this lie of Molly's, which was really as Bare-
Faced as the ones my sister had been telling
about being the owner of Honey instead
of me, but it had to be part of the plan to

make sure that Nick did actually get here while April was still watching telly. I crept into the sitting room to check that April was indeed still there, and she'd actually fallen asleep in front of an old black-and-white film, and was still wearing her beard!

Molly and I sat in the kitchen with Honey and waited for the Masterly Plan to take effect. We decided to pass the time by doing a bit of training with Honey. I had not really done much of this up to this point, as Honey was still so tiny.

We flicked through the *Love Me, Love My Dog* book until we found the section on training. It was very useful as the author, Monica Sitstill, had divided all the different training commands up into little sections so that you could easily find the bit on 'How to Make Your Dog Sit' or 'How to Make Your Dog Stay' and so on, etc.

'Let's try and get Honey to understand the "sit" command first,' said Molly. She always takes charge when we are together, and sometimes I find this annoying, but this time she was doing me an extremely Good Deed by helping me with her Masterly Plan, so I decided I wouldn't find it annoying this time.

'I'll get some of the treats we bought her,' I said as Molly read aloud from the book about what we had to do.

'"First make sure you have a tasty treat in your hand,"' she read.

'Check!' I said. I like using that word like that, because it is what they say on those programmes when people are in aeroplanes and are checking important items off a list before they go on a secret mission.

'"Call your dog,"' Molly went on.

'Honey!' I called.

Honey was already lying at my feet, so she couldn't come to me. She put her head on one side, but didn't get up or anything.

Why call me? I'm here already.

Molly read out the next bit: '"Show your dog the treat. Let him [or her, of course] sniff it, but don't let him [or her] eat it."'

Ha! Easier said than done. The minute I showed Honey the treat, she snatched it and gobbled it up.

Yum! Snack time!

Molly sighed and said, 'Get another treat and try again. This time, wait till Honey's

157

standing up and then hold the treat just
above her nose so that she has to tip her
head back to look at it. Monica Sitstill says
that this will make the dog sit and then you
can say "sit" and give Honey the treat the
moment she sits.'

I tried again. Honey was standing now
and watching the biscuit with a beady,
greedy look in her eye. I held the biscuit
above Honey's head. She jumped up
and snatched it again before I could say
anything at all.

This is my kinda game!

I was starting to get quite fed up with
Honey. And Molly was starting to get quite
fed up with me.

'You're not concentrating, Summer,' she
said in her bossy voice, which always makes

me feel like I don't want to carry on playing with her any more. I did my best to take a deep breath and Not React, which is what Mum is always advising me to do when April annoys me.

I took another treat and held it over Honey's head again, but this time I held on to it very tightly as there was absolutely no way I was going to let her snatch it. She looked at the biscuit and I moved it a bit further back over her head so that she had to tip her head back like it said in the book. I said 'sit!' and she sat!

I fed her the treat, then Molly and I whooped and jumped around and said, 'Good dog! Good dog, Honey!'

Look at you, leaping about all over the place. I only sat down. You guys get excited over the weirdest things . . .

But, hey, you want to jump and whoop now? OK, I'm up for a bit of jumping and whooping!

Honey started jumping and whooping too — well, yapping anyway, and we were having so much fun we nearly didn't hear the front doorbell ring.

But luckily we heard it just in time and luckily April heard it too and woke up with a start and ran to answer the door, which was all part of Molly's Masterly Plan.

'Oh, er, hello,' said a voice, which was most definitely Nick Harris's beardy voice.

'Hi!' said April. We were spying on her from behind the kitchen door. She was doing the hair-flicking thing, which obviously meant she was pleased to see him.

'Erm, I got a call to say that Honey was ill,' said Nick Harris.

Me? Ill? I've never felt better! The blonde with the beard's not looking too hot though . . .

Nick was talking in a hesitant sort of manner and looking at my sister in a funny way, and it was no wonder because she was STILL WEARING THE BEARD!

But of course, she had not realized that she was. Molly and I were trying very hard indeed not to have one of our giggling sessions. I leaned a bit further out of the kitchen so that I could get a good view of what was happening at the front door.

'Oh, I don't think so,' said April, and then she said, 'but why don't you come in and have a cup of tea?'

'N-no, I won't, actually,' said Nick Harris, holding his hand out in front of him and backing off down the driveway as if my sister was a dangerous animal he was trying to get away from very quickly indeed.

'Oh, OK, if you're sure?' said my sister, flicking her hair in a quite desperate manner.

'Yes – thanks – I'm sure!' Nick Harris shouted and he broke into a run as he got closer to his car. He fumbled with the keys

and dropped them. He did look
really quite panicky, and although it
was funny and Molly's Masterly Plan had
obviously worked in a truly masterful way, I
did begin to feel a little bit guilty that Nick
Harris was looking so freaked.

April shrugged and closed the door. As
she did so, she caught sight of her reflection
in the mirror and saw . . . THE BEARD!

'Oh, Argh! EEEEEK! OH NOOOOO!'
she cried. Then very unfortunately for us,
Molly and I could not hold in our giggling
any longer and some giggles spilt out and
April heard us.

She turned on her heel, ripping the beard
off her face as she did so and bellowed in
an extremely loud voice:

'YOU'LL REGRET THIS, SUMMER
HOLLY LOVE – YOU MARK MY
WORDS!'

She actually looked a bit like a cross
between Monica Sitstill and Mr Elgin and I
was actually quite scared.

Molly was still giggling behind the door
though and whispered, 'I don't think we'll
be seeing any more of Mr Nick Harris
– or his beard! One vet well and truly
desensitized.'

No more Mr Hairy Guy!

13

How to Find Your Puppy Love

April told Mum about the Beard Episode later that day. I could tell that Mum wanted badly to laugh long and loud about it, but she could obviously tell that April very much did *not* want her to, so Mum did not. But her mouth twitched a lot at the corners, and her face went quite beetrooty.

April stormed up to her room and said she was going back to work the next day as it would be more of a holiday than being at

home with me in This Madhouse. She also
told Mum that we should never have got
Honey because she was a Liability. She said
that I would never make a good dog owner
because I didn't care about Honey's behaviour
and that we would all 'Live To Regret The
Day That Mutt Ever Set Foot In This House'.

 Who's she calling 'Mutt'?

All this was so unfair, because the only
thing Honey had done wrong so far was
not like a man with a beard that my sister
happened to be in love with.

When April had gone to work the next
morning, I told Mum this.

Mum said, 'I know that your sister is
being unfair, not to mention a little strange,
but that's what being in love does to people,
I'm afraid.'

I said that in that case there was no way in the history of the world, or indeed the universe, that I would ever fall in love with anyone. *Ever.*

Mum smiled and gave me a hug. 'You love Honey though, don't you?' she said.

'Don't be daft, Mum. That is *no way* the same thing,' I said, rolling my eyes. Honestly, Mum is on such a different wavelength most of the time I wonder how she ever manages to cope out there in the Big Wide World.

'Of course, Summer. I know that,' said Mum. 'But I was just thinking, well, maybe April's just a bit upset because you've got Honey and you're really happy about that, but she can't seem to get Nick interested in her and *she's* really unhappy about *that*. So maybe you should help her.'

I didn't understand this at all. 'Mum,

if Nick Harris doesn't like April, there's nothing *I* can do about it,' I explained patiently.

Mum smiled again. 'Wouldn't you like it if April stopped trying to come between you and Honey?' she asked, sounding almost as patient as I did.

'Hmm,' I replied. I didn't know what Mum was up to, and I didn't want to be too enthusiasticated in case it was something dodgy.

'Well, I have a theory,' Mum went on, her eyes twinkling with mischief in a very un-Mum-like way. 'If we can engineer things so that Nick and April get together for a date, I think I can guarantee that April will lose interest in Honey overnight.'

I pulled the face that Molly calls my Dubious Expression, which is when I turn down the corners of my mouth and raise

my eyebrows to show that I
am unsure about an idea.
Still, maybe Mum
had a point. Maybe
if April got
together with
the love of her
life, I would be
left in peace
and quiet with the
love of mine – that
is, Honey.
'OK,' I said.
'But how are we
going to engineer things like that?'

Mum grinned. 'First we need to arrange
for Nick and April to bump into each other
without Honey being there,' said Mum.
Her eyes looked a bit crafty now and less
twinkly. 'I think I can organize something,'

she continued, 'but you've got to keep shtum,' she added, which I guessed must be Mum's way of saying it would be a secret from April.

She went on to unfold her Masterly Plan. Honestly, everyone seemed to be having Masterly Plans apart from me. I just had to cross my fingers and toes and hope to high heavens above that this one would work . . .

That evening, Mum put one of her most delicious-looking lasagnes in the oven. On the dot of six o'clock April walked through the door. Her lasagne-radar-smell-o-vision was obviously working.

Mm-hmmm! She's not alone there.

'Nice day, dear?' asked Mum.

'Yeah, great to be out of this madhouse,' said April. 'Is it lasagne for tea?'

'Yes, but unfortunately Summer and I won't be able to stay and have it with you,' said Mum.

'Oh?' I could tell April was still very miffed with me and Mum and the Whole World in General as she often is when only one person has upset her and she decides to let everyone in the nearby VICINITY know about it.

'Yes, er, Summer and I have decided to go to the town hall this evening to a new dog-training class that we've only just found out about,' Mum said. I didn't think she sounded like she was being very convincing or truthful, but April didn't seem to notice. 'We'll be out for a couple of hours – with

Honey too, of course,' she added. Then she beckoned to me, grabbed the dog lead and her coat and, taking me by the hand, she almost ran out of the house.

'Don't bother saving us any lasagne!' Mum called as we ran to the car with Honey. 'We'll grab something in town.'

 Hey! Don't listen to her! That lasagne had my name on it.

I wondered whether April would think it was odd that Mum had laid two places for tea.

Mum and I went to the park and played a bit with Honey. She'd packed us some sandwiches so we ate them while Honey chased butterflies and bees and made us laugh.

You guys are easy to please!

After a while Mum said she thought it would be fine to go home, so we did. I was hoping that April would be in a better mood now that she had had the house to herself for a bit and that there was lasagne for tea.

As it turned out, she was in a much better mood, but I don't think it had much to do with the lasagne.

When Mum and I walked into the kitchen, April was still sitting at the table. She had a man with her who I didn't recognize. I was rather a bit perplexed as this man definitely wasn't Nick. What was my strange sister up to now? Had she just gone and wrecked Mum's Masterly Plan by falling in love with a different person?

Then April looked up and said, 'Hello!'

The man turned round and said, 'Hello!'
too, and I thought, I recognize
that voice, but I still don't recognize the
face.

'You don't recognize me, do you,
Summer?' said the man.

Then I realized – and I nearly fainted,
which would have meant I was beginning
to make a habit of it, so I'm very extremely
glad I did not.

It was Nick Harris!

With no beard!

Honey rushed over to him and licked his
hand.

'That's better,' said Nick. 'You like me
now, don't you?'

NO idea who you are, But you
sure smell good!

174

April was blushing very much indeed, and Mum was smiling a lot.

'Why haven't you got a beard?' I asked. 'Was this part of your plan, Mum?'

'Summer!' she hissed.

'What plan?' asked April.

'Nothing,' said Mum and started to rummage about in the cupboard as if she was looking for something very important and simply didn't have time to answer any questions.

Nick laughed. 'No, Summer, your mum didn't have anything to do with me shaving off my beard! I just realized that it was – how shall I put it? – coming in between me and someone I quite liked.'

He was patting Honey's head as he spoke so I asked, 'What, you mean, you and Honey?' I felt quite a bit panicky and I hoped he was not going to take my beautiful puppy away from me.

'NO! Well, not really,' Nick answered. 'I wanted to see your sister again, but I could tell that Honey wasn't going to let me near her as long as I kept my beard. It's quite common for new puppies not to like men with beards.'

I had a sudden thought. 'Mum, did you *tell* Nick why we bought the beards?' I asked.

April did not seem to appreciate me mentioning the Beard Episode again. She jumped up, knocking the rest of the lasagne on to the floor.

At last – the moment I've been waiting for!

'Don't worry, April,' said Nick. 'If it wasn't for your mum, I wouldn't be here tonight.'

176

How to Find Your Puppy Love

April was speechless, which I think is the very first time in her life since I have known her that she has been.

Nick explained that Mum had called to say that Honey was ill and that this time it was real and could he please come round after six o'clock to see her. Nick had of course said yes, because he is a very professional and caring vet who loves dogs, even dogs who don't like him and who live in houses with Bearded Ladies.

He had turned up to find that Honey wasn't there – only April, who invited him in to apologize about the Beard Episode, and they had ended up eating the lasagne together, which is of course exactly what Mum had wanted them to do. They had had a lovely evening and had agreed to see each other again at the weekend. April started blushing again when Nick said this last bit.

177

'But I still don't understand why you don't have a beard any more?' I said.

Nick blushed this time, and because he didn't have a beard any more, you could see all of the blush.

'I shaved it off,' he said.

'Well obviously,' I said. 'But why?'

'Because I didn't want April's puppy to freak out at me,' he explained. 'After I saw April wearing a false beard, I thought about why a beautiful girl would go around wearing a beard and then I remembered that Honey had got really upset both times she had seen me at the surgery, so I thought maybe April was trying to get Honey used to seeing a beard. Some of those dog books suggest it as a way of desensitizing your dog,' he added. 'So I thought, April won't bring Honey to see me again if Honey doesn't get used to beards, and if April doesn't bring her puppy to see me, I won't get to see April . . . And so, I shaved off my beard.'

By this time, Nick and April were both grinning and blushing so much they looked like a pair of CERTIFIABLE lunatics and I felt like I wanted to just turn around and leave them both to it. Then I suddenly realized what an AWFUL MISTAKE Nick Harris had just made. I had to put him straight once and for all before disaster struck . . .

'Honey is MY puppy, not April's!' I cried.

Yeah – you're the mummy!

'Oh,' said Nick Harris.

'Yes,' I said in a firm and stern tone, 'April only *pretended* Honey was hers so that she could get to meet you properly after she

saw you in town and liked you and found
out where you worked.'

Mum stepped in to De-Fuse the Tension
at this point, except she obviously couldn't
think of a funny jokey way to do it so she
just said, 'All's well that ends well,' which
was pretty lame, I thought. 'Nick and April
are together, and April will leave you and
Honey to it from now on, I'm sure,' Mum
added.

Luckily Nick seemed to think that Mum
had actually told a hilarious joke anyway –
either that or he was good at playing along
at the whole De-Fusing the Tension idea –
so he laughed. And then April laughed. And
then, bizarrely, I started to see the funny side
of the whole embarrassing Beard-Puppy-
Confusion-Love-Story thing, and I laughed
too.

Since that very day, Nick and April have

continued to be NAUSEATINGLY loved-up. And this is very fine by me, as Honey is now totally and absolutely
MY PUPPY again,

and I must admit that I am quite loved-up with her too. Although not nauseatingly so. At least, I don't think so. And Molly comes round all the time and is Second-in-Command with everything to do with Honey. Even though I know she would prefer to be First-in-Command.

So that's the story of how my wish came true and I got my Puppy Love and how my sister nearly wrecked my wish by claiming my puppy as her own while behaving totally weirdly and frankly mega-embarrassingly . . . But how she, in the end, got her love too!

Don't you just love
a happy ending?

Bringing a Puppy Home for the First Time

Extract from *Love Me, Love My Dog* by Monica Sitstill

aka the Guru of All Things Dog-Related

Before you bring a puppy home, you should ask yourself some serious questions.

This is 110% true: my life will never be the same now I have my Puppy Love

Your life will change forever when you welcome a dog into your home, and it will be difficult to appreciate quite how true this is until the day your pet comes to stay.

And imagine if the dog peed when you were only halfway down the stairs!

For example, if you have never had dogs before and you live, let's say, in a fifth-floor flat in a city centre, you should not even think about getting a puppy. How are you going to house-train him? You will have to walk up and down those stairs a lot to take him out to pee.

Here are some further important points to consider carefully:

🐾 In the early stages of puppyhood, dogs are very demanding. Someone must be at home all the time to cope with house-training, and also to ensure the dog feels safe and secure in his new environment.

It certainly was hard work. Actually, Mum said it was Exhausting and Wearing and Blinking Messy.

🐾 A dog must be exercised regularly.

🐾 Two walks a day is ideal, but one long walk is acceptable as long as the dog has time off the lead to run around. However, a dog should never be left to run off unsupervised in case he hurts himself – or someone else.

These are what Molly would call Exceptionally Wise Words. As Honey got bigger, she ~~certainly~~ certainly got into various situations of quite a picklesome nature.

Most important of all: DOGS NEED TRAINING.
It is never too early to start training your puppy. Otherwise even the cutest, most friendly of dogs can turn into a monster. You'll need a lot of time and patience.

I AM SICK OF BEING IGNORED EVERY TIME I TELL HONEY TO SIT.

Anna Wilson, who is the actual author of this book, was never that fond of dogs. She was always a definite cat-type person. So she got two black cats called Ink and Jet and thought that would be that in the Pet Department of her life. But then the dog-type person she was married to (called David) decided that enough was enough and it was time he Had His Way For A Change, and the two children (called Lucy and Thomas) said that actually they thought dogs were quite a good idea too. So Anna Wilson sighed heavily and said she supposed she would have to Give In to the Whole Dog Idea.

That was when Kenna, the gorgeously soft, sweet and funny black Labrador puppy, came into her life and turned it inside out and upside down ... With the entirely surprising result that Anna Wilson is now very definitely and quite simply a **CAT-AND-DOG-TYPE PERSON!**

Moira Munro, the illustrator of this book, is pitifully allergic to furry animals. It is a Terrible Tragedy not to have a pet to stroke. Luckily, Moira Munro does have a daughter (called Chloe) who is at least as snuggly as a Labrador pup. Children are easier to look after than puppies because you can attach a nappy to them. Children can also, after a few years, do your work for you. Moira Munro still owes Chloe **£1.99** for writing out Summer and Molly's list on page 56.

Anna Wilson

Pup Idol

In our next truly amazing book, Honey goes through her Awkward Adolescence – in other words, develops a taste for shoes (mainly flip-flops), and for raiding our fridge and terrorizing dinner guests. Mum is not particularly delighted so Steps Have To Be Taken and eventually, with a bit of dutiful training, Honey develops true Star Quality and we all become Famous Celebrities in Our Own Right at the school talent show.

Available now in all good bookshops!

Anna Wilson

Puppy Power

I never thought I would say this, but life with Honey, my Number One Pooch, had been getting a little bit yawnsome of late. She was still 110 per cent gorgeous, of course, but now that she was TREMENDOUSLY well trained by me, there wasn't exactly much happening in my life on a day-to-day basis.

That is, until Nick Harris, Mr Fantabulous Vet of the Year, came up with the idea of Honey having PUPPIES . . .

Fairy Stories

Chosen by Anna Wilson

Every fairy has a story to tell

Be spirited away to fairyland and visit the wonderful
worlds of dream fairies, funny fairy godmothers,
a sweet-toothed cake fairy and a fairy who learns
a *lot* about friendship.

This magical story collection is a must for all fairy fans.

Princess Stories

Chosen by Anna Wilson

A pretty-perfect princess and a badly behaved princess, a
princess in love and a princess in BIG trouble . . .

These are just a few of the princesses on parade in this
fun, magical story collection.

Anna Wilson

Kitten Kaboodle

Bertie Fletcher's Pet-sitting Service is open for business!

Lonely Bertie has only ever wanted one thing – a pet – but her grumpy dad won't even let her have a goldfish. So she secretly sets up her own pet-sitting business – and meets Kaboodle, the tiny kitten who lives across the road . . .

A funny, heart-warming and slightly cat-astrophic story about a kitten whose tongue is sharper than his claws!

Available now in all good bookshops

Anna Wilson

Kitten Smitten

What happens when two families are smitten by the same kitten?

With new pet Jaffa in her life, Bertie Fletcher is happier than the cat that got the custard. But then the annoyingly perfect Meerley family arrives on the scene and threatens to lure 'Muffin' away in a dramatic tug of love. May the best family win . . .

A hilariously zany story about a cat with too many owners on her paws!

Coming to all purr-fectly good bookshops in February 2010

A selected list of titles available from Macmillan Children's Books

The prices shown below are correct at the time of going to press. However, Macmillan Publishers reserves the right to show new retail prices on covers, which may differ from those previously advertised.

Anna Wilson

PUP IDOL	978-0-330-45290-8	£4.99
PUPPY POWER	978-0-330-45291-5	£4.99
KITTEN KABOODLE	978-0-330-50771-4	£4.99

Chosen by Anna Wilson

FAIRY STORIES	978-0-330-43823-0	£4.99
PRINCESS STORIES	978-0-330-43797-4	£4.99

All Pan Macmillan titles can be ordered from our website, www.panmacmillan.com, or from your local bookshop and are also available by post from:

Bookpost, PO Box 29, Douglas, Isle of Man IM99 1BQ

Credit cards accepted. For details:
Telephone: 01624 677237
Fax: 01624 670923
Email: bookshop@enterprise.net
www.bookpost.co.uk

Free postage and packing in the United Kingdom